Peter's New Home

Sheila Hollins, Nigel Hollins, Deborah Hutchinson and David Towell
illustrated by Beth Webb

Beyond Words

Leatherhead

1

3

VAO 386

VAD 386

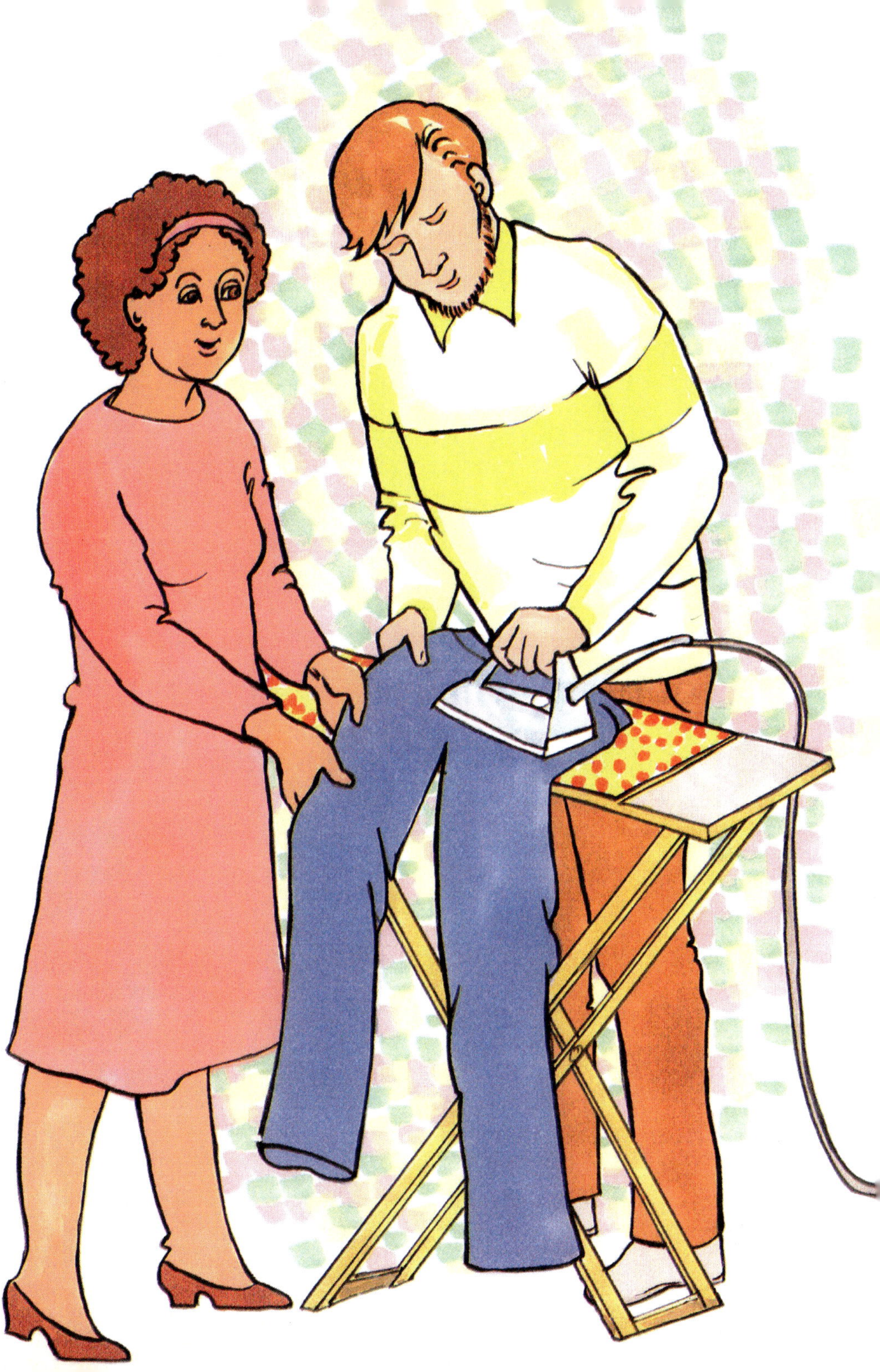

27

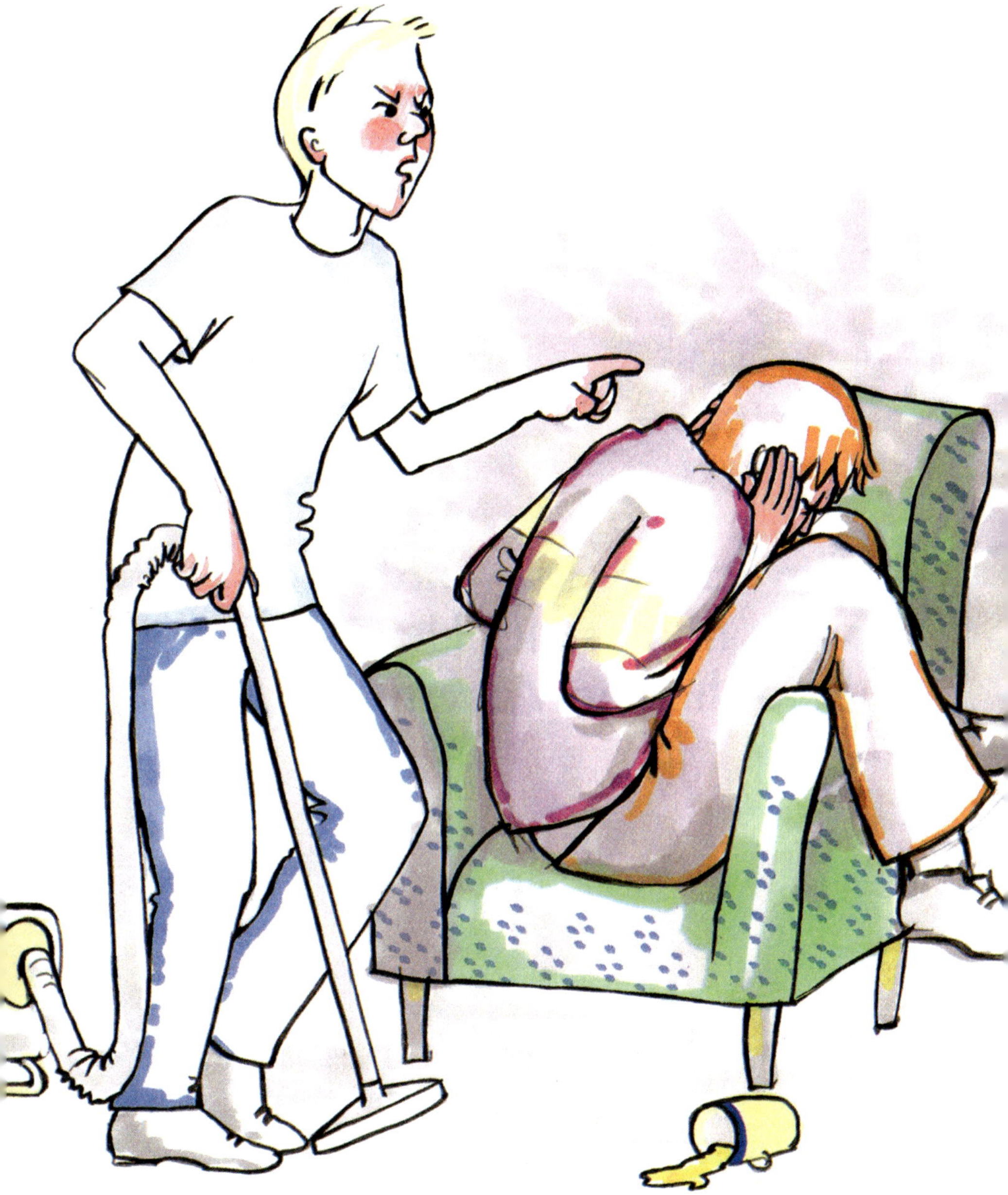

First published 1993, by St George's Mental Health Library. Second edition published 2015, Books Beyond Words.

Third edition published 2023, Books Beyond Words.

ISBN 978-1-78458-165-7

British Library Cataloguing-in-Publication Data

A catalogue record for this book is available from the British Library.

Printed by Royal British Legion Industries, Leatherhead.

Books Beyond Words is a Charitable Incorporated Organisation (no. 1183942).

Further information about the Books Beyond Words series can be obtained from Beyond Words' website: www.booksbeyondwords.co.uk.

More Information

https://booksbeyondwords.co.uk/s/BBW-Peters-New-Home-Resources